The Ogre On The Hill
And other stories

By Ray Newman

Enjoy
Ray Newman

Copyright © 2019 Ray Newman
All rights reserved.

Table of Contents

The Ogre On The Hill...............................3

The Old Farm Is Gone….AtLast......................17

Just Look for the Union Label.......................31

When God Created Choir Members...................43

Abe..46

A Shoemaker's Christmas...........................52

911..61

The Clock Maker...................................69

Smile..72

Mildred Hannibel...................................76

Money Isn't Everything.............................79

How The Wino Saved The World....................87

The Ogre On The Hill

Once, not so very long ago, in a castle on a hill, overlooking a small village, lived an Ogre. He was horribly ugly, as most Ogres are, but he had a kind and gentle heart.

A housekeeper named Gretta and a servant, Johann lived in the castle with the Ogre to care for him. And they loved him in spite of his ugliness because they knew he loved them.

Each day the Ogre would wander through the great castle, up and down the winding staircase, around the library full of wonderful books, into the kitchen where Gretta prepared such delicious meals and, finally, to stand at the window and watch the children of the village playing below. Often he would open the window just so he could hear their laughter.

"How lonely I am," he thought. "If only the children would come and play in my garden, and slide down my stairwell banister and have one of Gretta's wonderful sandwiches, then my loneliness would go away and this big old castle wouldn't be so silent.

But the children never came. For their parents had often told them of the Ogre and of his horrible ugliness and so they always feared the castle at the top of the hill and its lonely occupant.

One afternoon, in early spring, the Mayor of the little village stood at the window of his office watching dark clouds building beyond the hills to the West. "And now comes the rain," he said to himself. "From the look of those clouds there will be plenty." He turned from the window and went back to work at his desk.

The Ogre saw the clouds from his window as well. He stood and watched as they grew in size and began to race toward the valley. Soon the children would have to play indoors and he wouldn't be able to hear their laughter or watch their games.
Something about those clouds concerned him. They were much too dark, growing larger by the minute and a strong wind was driving them across the expanse from the hills to the valley.
"This looks like more than just a spring rain," he thought as he shut the window. "I think we are in for a terrible storm."

The mayor looked up from his desk as he heard the first drops of rain hit the window. It had grown much darker over the last few minutes and the wind had picked up. He heard the squeals of the children as the ran home, laughing and shouting at each other.

"Time for me to close up," he said. "I need to get home before the rain gets any worse." So he put on his coat, locked his office and started down the street. Suddenly there was blinding flash of lightning followed by a loud crash of thunder and the rain came in great waves across the valley.

The Mayor was soaked by the time he reached his front door where his wife was waiting.

"Hurry dear," she said. "Come inside and get out of those wet clothes. You should have taken your umbrella this morning."

The Mayor laughed. "I suppose you knew it was going to rain today."

"Well, it is Spring, you know." She turned and started for the kitchen. "I have water on for tea as soon as you've changed."

"I've never seen it rain so hard," The Mayor thought as he closed the door. "If it keeps up like this all night we may have some serious trouble.

"Would you like some tea, sir?" Gretta asked the Ogre as he sat reading by the fire.

"Yes, thank you, Gretta , that would be nice." He answered as he stood and moved to the window. It had grown dark and the rain still drove against the window with great force. "Have you ever seen a rain quite like this?"

"No, sir, never. And it scares me a little. I'm afraid for the village if the river starts to rise."

"The river? I never thought about that. The village is at the river's edge. If it overflows it could wash away the village."

Suddenly a great flash of lightning tore across the sky and the Ogre caught a glimpse of the river. It had already begun to rise.

"Come to bed, dear," the Mayor's wife called. "It's so dark you can't see anything out that window."

The Mayor stood for a moment longer then turned away. He draped his robe over a nearby chair and sat heavily on the edge of the bed.

"I think it's raining harder, if that's possible. I almost feel like I should stay up all; night."

"Can you stop the rain?" she asked. "Get some sleep. Everything will be fine in the morning, you'll see."

"I only hope you're right," the Mayor whispered to himself as he turned off the light.

Up at the castle the Ogre had fallen asleep in his chair with an open book laying across his lap. Gretta came in quietly and took the book. Laying it the table beside the chair she gently covered the Ogre with a blanket. He often fell asleep by the fire. Preferring to sleep there rather than in his huge, lonely bedroom. Then she tiptoed out.

A loud clap of thunder woke the Mayor from a fitful sleep. He got up quietly and walked to the window. The rain continued to beat down on the little village. "There's no let-up." He said to himself. If only it were light enough to see the river. I'm sure it must be rising fast."
As if in answer there was another blinding flash of lightning and for an instant the Mayor saw the river. His eyes widened in horror.
"The river," he shouted, waking his wife. "It's starting to overflow its banks. The village is in trouble."
He ran to the bed and grabbed his wife by the shoulders. "Quickly, get dressed and wake the children. The river is rising fast. I must warn the people. As soon as you and the children are dressed go to the Town Hall. It's on higher ground and we may be safe there."

The Mayor threw on his clothes, raced down the stairs and grabbed his raincoat. "I'm going to the chapel." He called out to his wife. "The Padre can sound the bell and wake the village. But I must hurry." With that he yanked open the door and stumbled out into the driving rain.

He could hardly see where he was going the rain fell so furiously. He had gone but a few yards toward the chapel when he realized he was ankle deep in water. "The river is rising faster than ever. There isn't much time."

At last he was at the chapel. He charged up the stairs and began banging loudly on the heavy oaken door. The Padre was an old man and a sound sleeper, but the hammering finally woke him.

"What it is?" Cried the Padre as he yanked open the door. "Why are you waking me at this strange hour. Is the village on fire?"

"In this rain?" Cried the Mayor. "What fire would stand a chance. No, no. The river is rising fast and the village is in danger. Sound the bell and wake everyone. Then get dressed and come to the Town Hall as quickly as you can."

With that the Mayor ran off down the street shouting at the top of his voice. "THE RIVER IS RISING! THE

TOWN IS IN DANGER! WAKE UP. WAKE UP. YOU MUST SAVE YOURSELVES!"

The Padre began to ring the bell in the chapel and it rang out over the village in spite of the driving rain and soon lights began to come on in all the houses.

Windows were thrown open as the Mayor ran up and down the village streets shouting his warning. At first they thought he had gone crazy from the rain but in the lightning flashes they could see the river was over its banks and the streets were filling rapidly with water so they turned quickly to the task of saving themselves.

And the chapel bell continued to ring.

The Ogre slowly opened his eyes. It was dark in the great hall with just a flicker of light from the dying embers in the fireplace. He could hear the rain beating against the window, and, softly in the distance, another sound.

"What's that? It sounds like a bell ringing." He got up from the chair and walked to the window. The sound was louder there.

"It's a bell. The bell of the chapel in the village. " He went to the great oak door and pulled it open. The sound was much louder now. He was right, it was the chapel bell. And as lightning flashed across the sky he saw the reason for the bell. The river was flooding the village. There was no time to lose.

"GRETTA…JOHANN…get up, get up. The village is in trouble." He shouted as he ran up the great curving staircase. Just as he reached the top the two servants came running from their rooms.

"What is it, Sir?" asked Johann. "Why are you shouting this way.?"

"The river is overflowing and the village is in danger. We must save them. Gretta, hurry to the kitchen put on several pots of your wonderful soup, and your sandwiches, yes, make lots of your sandwiches." Gretta hurried back to her room to dress.

"Johann, gather up all the blankets you can find, and dry clothing. Build up the fires in all the fireplaces for there will be many who will need to warm themselves." Johann turned and started for his room. Suddenly he stopped and turned back to face the Ogre. "Sir, how will you get the villagers to come here? You know they fear you greatly."

"No time to worry about that now. Just work quickly. I'll meet you downstairs. I'm going to the kitchen to help Gretta." He turned and bounded down the stairs.

The villagers were all in the Town Hall, huddled closely together, trying to comfort each other. The Mayor stood at the door with the Padre and another villager. They were watching the river creep closer to the steps.

"It's growing lighter," the Padre said. "Soon we can see the danger we face."

"Will that make it any easier to face?" the Mayor asked.

"No, my son," the Padre put his arm around the Mayor's shoulders. "It won't be easier. But you have done the best you could. Everyone is safe here."

"For now, but what about later?" The Mayor stepped out on to the porch. "Do you see how the river rises? If it keeps up we won't be safe, even here."

The three men stood silently and watched the river.

"Everything is ready." The Ogre stood at the door with Gretta and Johann. "Now we must go to the village and bring the people here."

"Sir, the people fear you. They don't know you like we do. Let Johann and I go and bring them here."

"No, it is my place to do this. I can't let either of you risk your lives."

"I will come with you." Johann was putting on his raincoat. "If they see me with you they may not be afraid."

The Ogre nodded his head. "You're right. But we must hurry. There isn't much time. The river is almost to the top of the Town Hall steps."

They started down the hill, slipping and sliding on the muddy trail. It had been years since the Ogre had been to the foot of the hill. The villagers had been badly frightened then. The Ogre only hoped their fear of the river was greater than their fear of him

The Mayor had gone back inside and closed the door. "Better for them that they don't see the river." He told himself. He wandered around the room, talking to the children, comforting the old people, strengthening the others.

And still the rain beat down.

The Ogre and Johann stood at the bottom of the steps to the Town Hall. The water was nearly to their knees. They looked at each other in silence, each knew what the other was thinking.

Then they turned as one and started up the steps.

The Mayor was kneeling near the door, talking to his oldest daughter, trying to calm her and her sister. His wife sat against the wall, hugging her knees, fear evident on her face. "The rain will stop soon, my dears," he told them. "Then the sun will come out and…"
Suddenly the door swung open. There outlined against the rain, stood the thing they feared more than the river. The Ogre had come. There was screaming as the villagers shrunk back in fear, afraid to face this terrible creature.
Only the Mayor stood between him and the people of the village. If necessary he would die to protect them.

The Ogre stood in the doorway and watched the villagers cringing in fear and loathing. "They will never come with me," he told himself "They fear my ugliness more than the river." But he held out his arms, and in a voice full of emotion, he spoke to them. "You must come with us. You are not safe here. The river will soon be high enough to wash away the Town Hall, and all of you with it. Come with us to the castle. There is food, and warm clothing, and a fire to keep you warm. But you must hurry."

The villagers stared at him in silence. This great ugly beast wanted to take them to the castle to save them. They couldn't believe it.

"Save us?" They cried. "Eat us, you mean. If we go to the castle we will surely be eaten. Here we only have to worry about drowning."

Johann stepped past the Ogre. "Listen to me. This man offers you safety, and the hospitality of his home. I have worked for him for many years. He does not eat people. He favors sandwiches. Come with us and save yourselves."

The villagers stood and stared at this Ogre they had feared for so long. No one moved. The only sound was the rain falling heavily on the roof.

"They will not come," the Ogre thought, "Their fear is too great. And I am too ugly. They would rather drown." And a tear grew at the corner of his eye and rolled slowly down his cheek.

Just then the Mayor's youngest daughter stood and walked up to the Ogre. The Mayor reached for her but she pulled away.

"Don't cry," she said. As she took his hand. I'm not afraid. Come Father, Mother, we will be safe at the top of the hill." And she climbed into the Ogre's arms.

The Mayor hesitated for only a moment, but the tear and the concern in his voice convinced him. He turned toward the villagers.

"Come on, what are you waiting for. There is safety in the castle. Hurry, the river is nearly to the top of the steps. Hurry. Hurry." And the Mayor gathered up his older daughter, took his wife by the arm and started after the Ogre. Johann reached down and lifted another small child into his arms and soon the whole village was slipping and sliding up the hill toward the castle. The Ogre ran back and forth along the line, hurrying them, helping those who fell, encouraging them, until at last they were all safely inside the castle.

The Ogre heaved a great sigh as he shut the heavy oak door and set about helping Gretta and Johann. For two days and nights the rain fell and the village was washed away by the raging river. But the villagers were safe and warm.

And the Ogre was thrilled to have so much laughter and excitement inside the old castle. And, though he stayed to himself he enjoyed having so much company. One morning the Ogre stood at the window and watched as the rain fell. "I think it is starting to slow down." He said to himself. "Soon it will stop and the people will set about rebuilding the village and they will be too busy to come see me." He sighed, "And I will be lonely again." And a tear formed at the corner of his eye and rolled slowly down his cheek.

"Why are you crying, sir?" It was the Mayor's youngest daughter. "Are you sad?"

"Yes," said the Ogre as he kneeled down in front of her. "I will miss you all when the rain stops and you are gone away."

The little girl reached up and took his ugly face into her hands. "Don't worry. I'll come visit you every day. And I will bring my friends and we will play in your garden."

"And will you have some of Grettas wonderful sandwiches with me, too?"

The little girl hugged him. "Yes, yes we will. And we will let you read us stories from the books in your big library."

"And will you slide down the bannister of the great staircase?"

"Oh, yes. Yes we will."

With that the Ogre scooped the little girl up in his arms and went dancing through the castle to the laughter and happy shouts of the villagers.

Gretta and Johann stood at the door of the kitchen and watched the fun.

"Well, Gretta. It looks like the curse of the Ogre is broken." Johann laughed.

"Yes, forever, I am sure." And they went into the kitchen to prepare more of Gretta's wonderful sandwiches while the children, led by the Ogre danced happily around the castle.

And nobody even noticed when it stopped raining.

****

The Old Farm Is Gone…At Last

"Francis?"

Ellie always called him Francis. She knew he preferred Frank. It was what his friends called him. But for all the years they had been married she had always called him…

"Francis? Could we…please…go out…to see the…old house…again?

Her words came much slower since the stroke, and her face showed the effort it took for her to put together the simplest of sentences. But Frank was a patient man and he always waited for her to finish.

"Oh, Ellie, why do you always ask to see the old house? You know they're probably tearing it down right now."

They had sold the old farm about a year ago, just after Ellie had recovered enough from the stroke to leave the hospital. It had been their home for thirty-seven years.

They had bought it with every penny they could scrape together and it nearly broke his heart to let it go. But, he wasn't a young man anymore and without Ellie to help him it would have been too much. So they finally gave in to the developer that had been after them to sell.

"I…know that, Francis…but I would just…like to see it …again. Could you…take me there…please?"

Alright, dear." He could never say no to her. "We'll drive out right after I clean up these dishes."

Frank got up from the table and took the napkin from under Ellie's chin. She reached up and gave his hand a feeble squeeze. He eased her wheelchair back from the table pushed her into the living room of the small home they had bought with some of the money from the sale of the farm. They hadn't ever been able to save much but they did get a good price from Mr. Anderson. In fact, some said it was more than the old place was worth. Frank didn't know about that. How do you put a price to thirty-seven years of work?

"You sit right there, honey, and I'll get the kitchen cleaned. Then we'll be on our way." He glanced out the window at the bright sunlight filtering through the trees across the street. "Sure looks like a nice day for the drive."

He left her sitting there, her hands folded in her lap, and went to the kitchen. Ellie had never let him help her with anything there when she was well. "You have your work," she would say as she pushed him out the door, "and I have mine."

She was a fine cook and housekeeper, and a caring wife and mother. They had raised three children on the old farm. Two sons and a daughter. Good children they were, too. Every Christmas they would all get together, along with the Grandchildren, to open presents and have a big dinner.

"I don't know what we'll do this Christmas," Frank

thought. "This little place isn't anywhere big enough for all that bunch."

Frank finished clearing the table and stacked the dishes in the sink. It would take some time to get Ellie ready for the drive, and he could always clean them when he got back. He took off the little apron he wore and draped it over a chair. He wore the apron because it made Ellie smile to see him in it.

"Well, that's all done," he laughed as he wheeled her into the bedroom. "I always thought you women had a tough job, but you were foolin' me all along." He liked to kid her about how well he did in the kitchen.

"Now Francis…you know that…if I had …my way you would never…see the inside…of that kitchen." She still hadn't accepted the fact that there was little hope she would ever be able to do much but sit and watch him do the things she felt were hers to do.

"I know, honey. I'm just teasin' you." He rummaged through the closet for something cheery for her to to wear. "Might help her spirits," he thought. He selected a bright pink dress that she had bought in St. Louis a few years back, when they had brought in a better crop than usual, and laid it out on the bed.

"That's a pretty…dress, Francis. I…remember…when I bought it. Oh, could I…wear the white…sweater, too?"

She wore a sweater most of the time now. Cold bothered her even when she was well.

Frank began removing her housecoat and nightgown. She could move a little and so she helped him as much as possible. It was a slow process, though. His hands were big, with a touch of arthritis, and so he had trouble with the snaps and things.

"I'm just not much good at this," he had complained the first time he tried to do it after she came home from the hospital. "I'm better at plowin' or fixin' the tractor." But he stopped complaining when he saw the tears in her eyes. He couldn't bear to hurt her.

Ellie had been the prettiest thing he had ever seen that day they first met. It was at a church picnic and he was new in town. He figured the best place to meet folks was at the church and the picnic gave him the chance. She was so tiny she looked like she would break if you squeezed her too hard. He found out later that she wouldn't.

Frank courted her for nearly a year before she said she

would marry him. But finally she agreed and they were married in that same little church. Now, almost forty years later, they seldom missed a Sunday. Although for awhile after her stroke Ellie wouldn't go.

Ellie's father liked Frank because he was a hard worker and after they were married he sold them the property they would spend nearly the rest of their lives on. Frank hadn't planned on being a farmer, but one year led to the next and pretty soon he realized that he was.

"I think…I would…like to…wear my pink…slippers…today. They…keep my…feet warmer…than any of…the others." Ellie was dressed, except for the shoes, and Frank was brushing her hair. This was the most enjoyable part of getting her ready to go somewhere. He loved to run the brush through her long hair. She had worn it long all through their marriage because she knew how much he loved it.

"Okay, honey. We'll be about ready, soon as I get my jacket." He stopped in front of her for a second. She seemed so small sitting there in the chair. She had lost a bit of weight the past few months but she was still the prettiest thing he had ever seen.

"Francis, you…stop staring at me…like that. I know…just how terrible…I look." She moved her hands in little flutters of agitation .

Frank reached down and caught hold of her hands, then leaned forward and kissed her cheek. "You never looked better, Ellie," he whispered. "You're more beautiful every minute."

She smiled then, and Frank went to the closet and put on his jacket. He wheeled her out to the porch and down the ramp he had built for her. It never was much of a job getting her into the car. She was so tiny he just lifted her up and into the seat as though she weighed nothing at all. He put the wheelchair in the trunk and went back to lock up the house.

Frank pulled the car out of the driveway and into the street. The drive would take them almost an hour, but it was one they had made all their lives while they lived on the farm. Since they had sold the place, though, they had only been back twice. Once to get some plants from Ellie's flower bed to put around the new place, and another time to get some fruit from the trees. Mr. Anderson had been very understanding and let them come back whenever they wanted.

"I'm not sure this is such a good idea, Ellie," Frank spoke softly. "I know how much you loved the old place. Do you really want to see it being torn down?"

Ellie sat quietly, and when she didn't answer Frank thought she must not have heard him. He was about ready to ask her again when she spoke.

"I want…to see the…place, Francis. It's…important to…me." She turned to look at him and there was a small tear at the corner of her eye.

"It won't be pretty, Honey. The bulldozers and all that will be making a big mess. Are you sure you're up to it?" Frank was worried that the strain would cause another stroke. He couldn't bear to think of going through all that again. He had nearly lost her. He had found her on the floor of the kitchen that afternoon. At first he thought she was dead but he managed to get to the phone and call for help. Then he went back to her, sat down on the floor, took her in his arms and started to pray. He was still praying when the ambulance arrived, and he never stopped praying until they told him she would be okay.

She had turned back to the window. "I'm…alright. I'm alright."

He looked at her out of the corner of his eye and thought, "Why does she want to go back now? It'll be hard enough for me to see the old place. I'm not sure what it will do to her." They were only about ten minutes from the place when Ellie spoke again.

"Francis…you really loved…that old farm…didn't you?"

"Why, sure, Honey. It was our home."

"But you…had to work so…hard…just to…make enough for…us to live on. Thirty-seven…years. That's a…long time."

Frank thought for a moment. "that's a lifetime, Ellie."

"Didn't you…ever get…tired?" There was more than just a question in her voice. "Didn't you…ever just… feel like…giving up?"

"Giving up, Ellie? That was all we had, that old farm. If I gave up we would have starved. You never gave up."

Ellie was silent. Frank was confused by all this. He had spent all those years trying to make the farm pay off, but it never did. Not until he sold it. But had he ever thought about giving up?

"You never gave up, Ellie. So I had to keep going too."

I…almost did, Francis. On…the floor…in the kitchen. I…almost…gave up…there."

Frank reached out his hand to her.

"But then…I heard you…praying …and well, I prayed, too. I…prayed we …could leave that…farm. I…prayed that we…could have…an easier…time. Mostly…for you, Francis. Mostly…for you."

Frank slowed the car for the turn onto the road that passed the old farm.

"And now, look…at us. I'm more…of a burden than… that old dirt farm…ever was. I…didn't want…it to be…like this, Francis."

The farm was in sight now. There were several pieces of equipment moving back and forth across the land, scraping dirt in mounds in some places and flattening it in others. Right in front of them was the old place. It looked so small now. Not like it had when they lived there. It was a big house then. Big enough to raise a family in.

"There it is, Ellie. I don't think we ought to get any closer." Frank pulled the car to the side of the road and switched off the motor. The sounds of the bulldozers invaded the quiet of the car.

"This is close…enough. I…can see fine…from here." She sat quietly, her hands folded in her lap, as the bulldozer worked closer and closer to the house.

"Francis…I'm glad we… are free… of that old… farm." Ellie's voice was firm.

"What? What are you saying, Ellie. That was our home. We worked hard to make it go." Frank couldn't believe his ears. All those years. Had she hated it so much?

I…watched you…waste your life…on that…good for nothing…pile of dirt. We…were young and…you were so…strong, and I…loved you so…much. I watched you…get old there." She turned toward him and reached out her hand to his. "I never…said anything… because I thought…it was what you…wanted. That farm…took you away…from me. I worked…beside you…because I loved…you. But…all the time I…saw it beating…you down."

"Ellie, I never knew. I thought…" His words were interrupted by the sound of metal tearing into wood. They both looked out to see the bulldozer as it crashed through the side of the house. The wood creaked and cried out as though it were alive. But the 'dozer soon finished the job and began to load the splintered wood into the back of a truck.

Frank and Ellie sat for awhile and watched the last of the old house being dumped into the truck. There didn't seem to be much to say. Ellie was the first to speak.

"Free."

Frank wasn't sure he heard her right. "What did you say, Honey?"

"Free. I said…free. The old place…is finally…gone… and we will never…have to go back…there again."

"Thirty-seven years is a long time to live with something you hate," Frank said. "Should have told me sooner. I worked so hard all those years because I thought it was what you wanted. I would have done anything for you, Ellie."

"Oh, Francis…how I hated to see…you grow…older. I wanted us…to be always…young. It's too late…now. I'm free…of that old…farm but…I'm still not…free." She lowered her head and Frank put his arm around her.

"I couldn't believe…that God …would answer my… prayer this way." She had started to cry. "How could I…trust God? He answered…my prayer…but not … like I had… hoped…or wanted."

"Ellie, don't." Frank tried to calm her.

"No… I have to tell… you. You have…to know. When I…left the hospital…I never wanted to…set foot in…a church again. You remember…how long it took…to get me…to go back…to get me…to go on…a Sunday?"

Frank nodded.

"I was so…full of hate…and every day…I saw…you giving…yourself to…me…caring for me…loving me. I almost came…to hate you." Ellie looked up at him. "You…never complained, you…never got angry, no matter…what I did. And…all the time…I kept asking…God…why…why…why?"

Frank wiped the tears from her eyes with his handkerchief.

"Then…one night I…heard you praying. I'm sure… you thought I…was asleep. You didn't ask…for a miracle…or help…or an end …to the pain. All…you asked for…was strength. Strength to be…able to do… for me as long…as I needed…you. I was…so ashamed."

Frank remembered that night. It had been a particularly tough day and Ellie hadn't made it any easier. After he got her into bed he knelt by the window and poured out all the pain and frustration that had been building. He prayed for strength, and understanding, and peace.

"I prayed…that night, too…Francis. I prayed…that God would…forgive me…after blaming Him for what had…happened. And I…prayed that He would…help me…overcome this…stroke and make…myself useful…to you again. I just hope…you will always…want me."

Frank lifted her face to his. "Honey the first time I saw you at the church picnic I said to myself you were going to be mine. But for all these years it's been the other way around. I've been yours. The way you are don't change nothin'." Frank held her closer.

"Francis, I…never told you…this but, at…the picnic that…Sunday…?"

"What about it, Honey?"

"I told…my father…that we were…going to get…married. He just…laughed…but I knew…I knew."

Frank kissed her on the lips. "It's time we were going home, Ellie."

They drove along in silence for awhile. There didn't

seem to be much to say.

"Francis?" Ellie spoke.

"Yes, Honey."

"Could we stop…at Johnson's for…an ice…cream cone?"

Frank chuckled. "We sure can, Honey. We sure can."

****

Just Look For The Union Label

Well, I guess you could say that it all seemed to fall apart about the time of the Vietnam War. You remember that one, don't you? Oh, too young, eh? Anyway, that was the first war ever fought in the living rooms of America, thanks to the "miracle" of television. Watching those boys dying in the jungles, without stirring musical background, and trying to eat dinner was a little more than most folks could stand.

The fun went out of war right there.

Wasn't too long until we had an all volunteer Army to go along with our all volunteer Navy, Air Force and Marines. The trouble with that was, we had to keep offering bigger and better benefits, higher pay, shorter hours, private rooms and no inspections, plus a whole lot more just to get people to sign up. The Reserves and the National Guard had it rough, too. No reason for anyone to join up since there wasn't any draft.

Then, some wiseguy got the idea that they ought to have a union.

Next thing we knew there was a union for every job in the military. The cooks and bakers culinary union. The Combat Engineer's Union, to go along with the Infantry Dogface Union…well, you get the picture.

It got so that a Company Commander couldn't order his men to take an objective without going through the shop steward. If it was raining, too hot, too cold or the objective just didn't seem worth the trouble then there just wasn't any way the union bosses would go along with it.

Mostly the officers and top enlisted men just gave up and resigned.

With all the officers and top NCO's quitting the

President had to appoint the union leaders to the Pentagon and the Joint Chiefs of Staff. Shop stewards took over the smaller units and each of the branches formed their own Guilds. The Medical Corps attached itself to the American Medical Society and the Corpsmen stopped going on maneuvers with the rest of the military because everyone knew doctors didn't make house calls.

Made it rough on the wounded, waiting for office hours.

Then some two-bit dictator in one of those South American countries got a bright idea and marched his troops onto one of our destroyers and took it over. It was a Saturday afternoon and all the sailors were on shore leave so it wasn't too difficult. When the Sailors got back and found out that they were without transportation back to the US of A where they could pick up their check they demanded to be flown home. The President suggested to the Naval Guild that it might be nice if they made some sort of effort to get the ship back. The Guild decided it wasn't in the scope of their labor contract.

Didn't surprise anybody when they called a strike.

The President refused to issue the order to fly the

sailors home but the Air Force Guild came to rescue of their brothers and flew several planes down to fly them back. They managed to get everyone home in the two planes that the dictator allowed them to use after he captured all the rest.

The President called an emergency meeting of the Joint Chief's to discuss the situation and get the military back to their jobs. All the Guilds were honoring the strike and the country was defenseless.

No one but the President showed up for the meeting.

Now, while all of this was going on those nasty fellas on the other side of the world were watching and waiting for their big chance. The Russian Premier called on the Chinese Chairman to discuss the time table for the invasion. Took them two days to get over laughing about the situation and joking about how easy it would be to defeat the US and get down to serious talk.

That was when they found out the still couldn't agree on anything.

The conference fell apart and the very next day they declared war on each other. The fighting went on for twelve years. Nearly 200 million of their people died, and famine and disease killed off another hundred million or so. The whole world watched and waited to see who would finally win but the war didn't show any signs of stopping.

In the summer of the thirteenth year Cuba sent in troops and occupied both countries.

Now that conflict didn't have much effect on things here at home except for some very grisly TV news reports. If you think the Vietnam stuff was bad… Anyway, Congress refused to even consider arbitration because the unions, who benefitted from the weapons and materials contracts, contributed so much money to their election funds that they wouldn't dare do anything to upset them.

The President had long ago resigned and went off to the mountains to fish. So the Teamsters had taken over the running of the country.

Made sense. They were running everything else, anyway.

With the Teamsters in charge there wasn't anybody to strike against so everyone went back to work. But by this time inflation was up to 78% and so the Monetary Guild cranked up their printing presses and ran off a whole batch of new money to pay the huge salary increases the Unions kept negotiating with themselves to keep up with the inflation that the raises…oh well, you get the picture.

Things were pretty well out of hand when a very amazing thing happened. Back in the seventies some real enterprising scientists at our National Aeronautics and Space Agency got the bright idea to send a space probe into deep space to try and make contact with other life forms that might be out there. It was a pretty fancy contraption with all kind of things inside, like recordings and letters and such. And on the outside was a diagram of our solar system. Sort of a road map for anyone to find us and make contact.

Bad thing about that road map, enemies can use it the same as friends.

The first spaceship landed, unannounced on the long abandoned pads at Cape Kennedy. The Air Force was on their annual Guild picnic and had no idea anyone was coming. By the time they realized they had visitors the entire facility belonged to the new arrivals.

A delegation of Union leaders entered the ship and never came out.

No one had any idea what was going on but there were ships landing all over the planet.

There was some resistance, but it didn't last long. Our military hadn't fought anything in so long they didn't know where to start.

More and more ships kept arriving and the Visitors, that's what everyone was calling them now, were hard at work joining them together to build larger and larger complexes. Great crowds of people stood at what they hoped was a safe distance and watched the building of the huge structures.

A few of the old time Union members noticed that they looked an awful lot like factories.

The first broadcast came on the seventh day after the landing had stopped. It was heard by everyone in their own language and it ordered the leaders of the people to report to the complex in their area. It was decided that if the Visitors wanted to talk to the unions they could just come to Washington and sit down like civilized people and discuss it.

When the deadline came and passed without anyone showing up the Visitors destroyed Chicago, Paris, Berlin, Tokyo and Peking.

The next deadline was announced and everyone was there at least four hours early. The meeting was very confusing and they had a lot of difficulty understanding what the Visitors wanted. In fact it was several hours before they realized that they were to become part of a large, interplanetary industrial complex. Materials would be shipped in from other parts of the galaxy and they would spend their time crating items that would be used on the home planet.

The shock was so great that took them all of thirty minutes to declare a general strike in protest.

The Visitors had given instructions on just how the work crews were to be organized and issued a reporting order to start work in two days. Well, have you ever tried to tell a Union man just how he should be organized, or when he should report to work? At the end of the two days there were large crowds of people outside of each complex shouting, waving signs and doing what they usually did during a strike.

Precisely at the two day deadline the Visitors took matters into their own hands.

You've heard about Union violence? The Visitors knew more about strong arm tactics and brutality than any Union member ever dreamed of. One hour and thirty minutes later the first work crews began assembling machinery and within half a day the newly completed items began moving toward the transport rockets.

The first shop steward to complain about the working conditions disappeared, instantly.

The Military Guilds joined forces and attempted to drive off the Visitors but they had spent too much time striking for higher wages and benefits and too little time learning how to fight. Soon those that weren't dead were toiling silently in the factories. Men and women worked side by side in true equality, eighteen hours a day for no pay. They received two meals a day, one at the start of the shift and one at the end.

Wasn't too long before they started dying off like flies.

Things went on like this for about two months when the first signs of resistance began. They were just little things; a loose nut, a twisted bolt, a missing part or some improper lubrication. Hard to put your finger on, difficult to deal with, but very effective. The Visitors were merciless in their attempt to deal with the problem, but the sabotage continued. Soon there were more defective items leaving the factories than those that were properly constructed.

The Visitors began to act a little frustrated.

Productivity fell sharply and quality control had become almost non-existent. There were so many complaints that an efficiency expert was sent from the home planet to set things right. He spent almost four and a half weeks trying to straighten out the mess but finally left, mumbling to himself. Things continued to get worse and the Visitors continued to become more and more confused and depressed.

Guess you could call it the first Interplanetary Work Slowdown.

Three hundred and twenty seven days after the first ship had landed the Visitors decided that the whole thing wasn't worth the trouble and began packing up to go home, wherever that was. They left all the manufacturing equipment because it was so fouled up they could never hope to make it functional again. They just packed up their suitcases, or whatever and blasted off without a word to anyone.

Really wasn't very polite of them,

And if the factories and equipment they left behind were a mess the social order was a shambles. The Unions, the only cohesive element from the time before the Visitors, were broken. Most of the leaders were dead, and the old alliances had disintegrated, leaving a society that was almost primitive.

Just the right conditions for a strong leader to emerge, right?

Well, not exactly. As it was there just didn't seem to be anyone around who wanted to be in charge of anything, let alone an entire country. After the initial shock of the Visitor's leaving folks just sort of went off and did their best to survive. They settled down in the towns and villages. Those that remembered how to farm took up the plow. Those that knew how to repair things went about repairing and rebuilding what was left after the destruction caused by the now departed Visitors. Nobody ever hurt anyone intentionally and people seemed more ready to help their neighbor than ever before.

One Sunday morning a few of the folks even got together for a Church meeting.

All over the world people went about the job of rebuilding. They worked hard, and long, and for little or no pay. But they were happier than they had ever been. Each person tried to give their best in whatever they did and it was almost as if a peace had settled over the entire planet. Oh, here and there somebody would shoot off their mouth about shorter hours and higher wages, but nobody paid any attention.

Mostly the loud mouths just shut up and went back to whatever it was they were doin'.

I guess you know the rest of the story about as well as I do. A few brave souls got together and started to put the country into some sort of order. They even went to what was left of Washington and found that old scrap of paper, dusted it off, made copies for each of their new states and posted it where everyone could read it.

The words were plain and simple, and most folks had no trouble at all understanding it. Some of them even went so far as to boast they had once known it by heart.

But I think the Constitution was a little too long for that.

While they were trying to get things goin' one of the people had the idea that they needed someone to be in charge of the whole country again. But there wasn't anyone around who wanted the job, or would have known what to do if he had it. Then they remembered that old President that had gone fishin' all those years back. They got in touch with him in those mountains where he had been livin' for so long and asked him to come back to his old job.

It took some persuadin', but I guess I'll give up fishin' just long enough to help them out.

****

When God Created Choir Members

Having created the heavens and the earth, all the animals thereof and mothers and fathers as well, the Lord decided to take a breather and work on something a bit simpler. Checking His list of projects He noticed one that He felt would be a cinch.

After all, there would have to be those who could sing His praises and gladden the hearts of His people when they gathered to worship. So He set to work creating choir members.

The project was two weeks old when Gabriel interrupted His work. "Lord, this has taken you longer than the creation of the entire universe. Is there a problem?"

The Creator looked up from His labors and shook His head. "I'm having a little trouble with the specifications. Mothers and fathers were a challenge, but how do I make a choir member?"

"Is this the spec sheet?" Gabriel asked, picking up a paper from the desk. "Let's check it out."

The Lord sat back in His chair as Gabriel began to read.

"First item, 'Must Love The Lord'." The angel smiled. "Well, that shouldn't be too difficult."

"You wouldn't think so," sighed the Almighty.

"Next item 'Must be committed'." Gabriel read on.

"Now there's part of the problem," God mentioned. "Not too many people are willing to give up their private time to attend rehearsal."

Gabriel shook his head. "Maybe you could modify that a little. You know, add something like, 'whenever they feel like it'."

"NO!" the Lord thundered, slamming His great fist down on the desk. "I won't compromise. It's the commitment that brings the joy."

Gabriel went quickly to the next item. "Size and Shape. Wait a minute, this says there is no requirement as to size and shape. Now that must be a mistake. I'll just call Quality Control and…"

"There's no mistake," the Lord interrupted. How can there be an accepted shape for a choir member? They come in an unlimited assortment."

Gabriel scanned the remainder of the list. "Well, there are only three more items on the Spec sheet and they all have the same notation, 'Sex, no requirement;' 'Color, no requirement;' and 'Voice, no requirement.' Wait a minute, surely there must be a requirement for voice?'

God smiled, and the Heavens radiated with the glory of it. ' Gabriel, you know that sex and color have never been important to me; what pleases me is the sound, especially when the effort is teamed with excellence. The quality of the individual voice is simply not important, only a willingness for each singer to do their best."

Gabriel was confused. Then what's the problem. Lord? The specifications seem so simple."

"I know, I know." He answered as He stood looking at the world He had created. "The problem is in finding enough volunteers to work with."

"Maybe if they knew how much it pleased you. More people would be available. Why don't you just tell them?" the angel suggested.

The Creator laid His hand on His Bible.

"I have," He said. "I have."

****

Abe

"Come right up here on the porch young feller. Have a seat in that rocker over there. It's right comfortable. Was my wife's favorite, rest her soul. Now, I don't get too many visitors here at the old place anymore these last few years. Used to be a regular stream of folks for awhile. But, time just seems to have passed me by. That's why, lately, I've been thinkin' that I wish that Booth feller had been a better shot.

"Oh, I'm sorry, I thought you knew. Feller's name was John Wilkes Booth. He was a right fair actor, but he hated me for one reason or another , so he set about to kill me. It was a good plan but he was better at actin' than he was at shootin'.

"Right after he grazed my temple with that one shot I saw him leap over the railin' at Ford's theater. That's where my dear wife and I were attendin' a play. Well, he hit the stage pretty hard and went limpin' out after he shouted some nonsense in some foreign language. Latin I think it was. If I had had the chance I would have thanked him for breaking up that awful play. It was almost as painful as the woundin'.

They took me across the street to Mr. Peterson's house to tend to the wound. Peterson was a pretty fine tailor, as I recall. He made me a suit a few weeks later, since the one I was wearin' sported a might of blood. And you know how hard that is to get out.

There was a bit of excitement in Washington that night, as well. Seems this here Booth feller had some friends that caused a bit of a stir but nobody was hurt too bad. And they caught up with him and a couple other fellers at a farm house and they all died in the fire that was set to smoke him out. After a few days things calmed down and I watched the war draw to a close just about a month after the shooting. Now I suppose that you would think that would have been the highlight of my time in office, and you probably would have been right, if so many other things hadn't occurred pretty soon after.

One of the real highlights, though, was the passin' of the thirteenth amendment, abolishin' slavery. But it seems like some things just die hard. Black folks that was expectin' to get their freedom found out it just didn't quite work that way. A bunch of die hards hid behind white sheets and called themselves the Ku Klux Klan. How's that fer a fancy name for folks who have hatred as their main emotion. They hung a lot of black folks, burned few of them at the stake and just generally spread a lot of terror. I sent the Army in to put them down and they went into hidin'. But, I understand they still put on those sheets and act like fools. And, of course, that and the war, earned me the undyin' hatred of a whole lot of fine Southern gentlemen who felt the blacks were only fit to be farm workers. It has been a comfort these last few years to see so many blacks climbin' out of that situation. Maybe another hundred years or so they will be able to vote, and buy their own farm, and go to school with the white kids. Might even get to be elected to President. Well, that might take more than a hundred years.

About a year or so after the end of our great war the whole European continent got into the middle of another big fight. Took everything I could do to keep us out of it.. France, and Italy and some of them other countries thought we would be a great help to them. But after the pain we had been through for five years I just flat out put my foot down and kept us right here in our own country, where we belonged. So I earned the undying hatred of a great many of those folks over there because I let them kill each other without any help from us. But, somehow, I have a hunch that sooner or later they will get after each other again, and we might not be able to stay out of it. I hope I'm wrong, but I bet I'm not.

One good thing about Mr. Booth bein' such a terrible shot. He has allowed me to see a great many things I would have missed out on. Like that feller Nobel, inventin' that explosive, what did he call it? Oh, yeah, dynomite. Strange name. Course he was a bit of a strange feller, too. Invented somethin' to blow people and things up, which I have seen cause a lot of sorrow these last few years, and then he creates a prize to honor people who, I guess, won't want to use his other invention. There was some talk of awardin' it to me one year. But all friends I made in Europe and the South put a stop to that pretty quick. But, over the years some mighty fine folks have gotten it.

And one of the biggest things about not sayin' goodbye to this old world back there in Ford's Theater is all the new stars that have been added to our flag. Each one a new state, and a new chance for folks to find a place of their own. Nebraska, North Dakota, South Dakota, Montana, Washington, Idaho, Wyoming and Utah. I was pleased to be a part of the purchase of the Alaska Territory. Lot of folks thought we were out of our minds, Mr. Seward and I. Seward's Folly, they called it. Personally, I think it was a bargain.

When my term was up my favorite General, Ulysses S. Grant, got elected to be the President. I would like to say he was a great President. Turned out he was a better General. He had a whole lot of trouble with public scandals during his first term. But the American people re-elected him to a second term in spite of it all. Guess they figured it couldn't get any worse. Of course, they were wrong.

So it has been a pretty excitin' time after all is said and done. Big strides in medicine, and technology. Speakin' of technology some feller named Bell invented this here contraption that lets you talk to somebody clear over on the other side of town, or even the country. I don't think it will catch on, tho. Writin' letters is so much more personal. Now, if they could figure out a way to write a letter and send it over that contraption, now that would be somethin'.

Oh, and did I mention the circus? Sometimes my memory fails me and I don't recall whether I've said somethin' before or not. Anyway, it was the first year for the Barnum and Bailey Circus. What a show. I had a box seat and got to stand up and wave at all the folks. Come to think of it, that was about the last time I ever got to stand up and wave at anybody, except the mailman as he passes the farm

There's been a bit of sorrow over these years to go with the joy. Buried my darlin' Mary a few years back. She never did get over the death of our boy, and her mind never was the same. She's at peace now. An assassin, who was a better shot than Mr. Booth, succeeded in killing President Garfield a few years back. And General Grant followed him not too far behind. Then, one of my favorite people died. Sojourner Truth. You say you never heard of her? Well, she was born a slave. But she didn't let that stop her. Got her freedom and became an Evangelist. Then spent the rest of her life fightin' slavery. I had the privilege of appointen' her the Commander to the Freedmen of Washington. She was a feisty lady.

And Frederick Douglas. Now, there was a feller who could talk the Angels right down from Heaven. He and I had many a spirited debate. He was a good friend. One of the few that continued to make regular visits out here to the farm. I miss him.

What's that? You say you have to be getting' along? Well, it's been a pleasure talkin' to you. I hope I haven't bored you too much. I just don't get many visitors any more. I guess I've just sort of faded out of the public eye. But then my time was a while back and it seems folks have short memories when it comes to ex-presidents. Like I said before, sure wish that Booth feller had been a bit better shot. Maybe old Abe Lincoln would be somethin' more than just a lonely old man sittin' and a rockin' waitin' to die. But that's the way life turns out sometimes.

****

The Shoemaker's Christmas

A long time ago, when shoes were still made by hand,
There lived in a village far away an old shoemaker

named Benjamin. But all the town folk just called him Papa Ben. He was quite happy, most of the time, and his eyes would sparkle and he would sing and whistle a merry tune as he worked. And he always had a cheery greeting for the people passing by.

But this day was different. This was Christmas Eve and the streets were mostly empty because everyone was home with their families. As Ben looked up and down the street he could see windows bright with candles and lamps shining brightly on the snow. He could hear the voices of children as they played in the snow.

"Ah, it's Christmas," he said to himself. "Everyone is ready to celebrate the birth of Jesus. He turned from the window and took a seat by the fire. On the table next to him was a Bible, which he loved to read. But he loved to read the story of the birth of Jesus most of all. So, picking up the Bible he turned to that story and began to read. He followed the words with his finger, saying the words out loud. "And she gave birth to her first born son, wrapped Him and swaddling clothes and laid Him in a manger, because there was no room for them at the Inn." Papa Ben paused and looked up from his Bible. "Oh my, oh my," He said to himself. "If Joseph and Mary had come here they could have slept on my good bed and I would have covered them with my patchwork quilt."

Ben read on. He read about the three rich rulers who came across the desert, led by a star, bringing wonderful gifts for the little baby Jesus. "Well, well," he said, "Wonderful gifts of gold and sweet smelling spices." Ben looked around his small shop. "If Jesus came here what could I give him?"

Laying down his Bible Papa Ben walked over to a shelf full of shoes and, picking up a small pair held them in front of him. "These are the best shoes I ever made." He said to himself. "If Jesus came these are what I would give Him." Pap Ben held the shoes close to his chest for a moment and the placed them gently back on the shelf. Returning to his chair he picked up his Bible again and continued to read.

Now Papa ben was an old man and, even though he loved the story he was reading, his head soon began to nod, his fingers slipped from the page and he fell fast asleep.

He hadn't been asleep too long when a voice woke him. "Papa Ben, Papa Ben," the voice called. He jumped from his seat and looked around to find where the voice came from. But he could see no one.

"Papa Ben," the voice continued. "You wished that you could see me. And that I would come to your shop so that you could give me a gift." Papa ben nodded his head, afraid to speak. "Well, keep watch on the street tomorrow and I will come. Watch all day from dawn to dusk and be sure to recognize me, because I will not say who I am. Then all was quiet in the shop.

Suddenly the church bells began to chime everywhere. Christmas had come.

Papa Ben slowly returned to his seat and picked up his Bible. "That was Him," he said as he closed the book and laid it back on the table. "That was Jesus. Or maybe it was just a dream," he said to himself.

"Well, no matter. I will watch and hope that He will visit me this Christmas Day." Then he stopped and scratched his head. "How will I know Him when He comes?

He got up from the chair and walked to the window looking out on the street. "He didn't stay a baby. He grew up to be a man, a king, they say. The Bible says that He was God Himself."

Ben turned away from the window, "Well, I shall be up early to be ready for Him when He comes."

***

Papa Ben didn't sleep much that night and he rose from his bed just before the sun came up, put on a pot of tea, moved his chair to the window and sat down to wait.

Suddenly he spotted someone on the street. He stood up, "Could it be Jesus, so early?" he thought. But no, it was an old man with a sack over his shoulder. One of the homeless that wandered the streets of this little town. Ben was a bit disappointed. He had hoped it was Jesus and they could spend the whole day together. The old man looked so cold and hungry that Papa Ben's heart was softened. He went to the door, opened it and called to the old man, "Friend, come in out of the cold and share a cup of tea with me, you look frozen."

"Are you sure," the old man said. "Many folks in this town say mean things and sometimes the children throw stones at me." Papa Ben just shook his head and brought the old man in, sat him in a chair by the table and brought him a cup of tea.

"I'm sorry about how some of the villagers treat you, but this is the least I can do. It is Christmas, you know." Papa Ben said as he returned to the window to watch for Jesus.

The old man sat sipping his tea and watching Papa Ben scanning up and down the street. "Are you waiting for someone," he asked. "I'm not in the way, am I?"

Papa Ben turned from the window, "Oh no, not at all. Have you heard about Jesus?" The old man nodded his head. "I have. That's what today is all about."

Papa Ben turned back to the window.

"He's coming today."

"You must be excited." The old man rose from his chair and put his cup on the table by the stove. "Thank you for the tea and a warm place to sit for awhile. I hope you will know Him when He comes." The old man picked up his pack and made his way to the street.

As Papa Ben watched the village began to come awake. As the townsfolk passed his window they all smiled and waved shouting a Merry Christmas to him. He smiled and waved back to each one as he returned their greeting.

It was then he noticed a young woman, carrying a baby. She looked very cold and the baby was covered by a thin blanket. Papa Ben went to the door and called to her.

"Come in. Come warm yourself and the child. A nice cup of tea will help and I have warm soup and bread."

The young woman came in and sat at the table as Papa Ben poured a steaming cup of tea. "Will you have some warm soup and bread?" he asked.

The young woman shook her head no and it was then that he noticed the baby had no shoes. "Your child has no shoes.

The young woman looked up with a sad smile, "I have none to give him."

Papa Ben's eyes lit up and he hurried to the shelf full of shoes and took down the small pair of handsomely made shoes.

Returning to the woman he handed her the shoes. "I think these will fit your baby."

"Thank you," the young woman said as she placed the shoes on her baby's feet. But Papa Ben didn't hear her. He had returned to the window. He was afraid Jesus had gone by while he was helping the woman.

"Is something the matter?" The woman asked. "Why do you watch the street so closely?"

"Have you heard of Jesus, who was born this day so

long ago?" Papa Ben spoke, not turning away from the window. "He's coming today and

I must keep watch for Him." He quickly told the woman about his dream. She listened politely until he had finished.

"I hope your dream comes true," she said, and with that she went on her way.

Hours passed and many people passed by Papa Ben's shop. Children, and old men, beggars and Grannies, cheerful people and grumpy people. To some he gave a smile and a greeting, to the beggars a coin or a hunk of bread.

But Jesus did not come.

The sparkle in Ben's eyes began to dim as he noticed the fog begin to envelope the village.

"It's late," Ben said. "And the fog has covered everything. I can hardly see the street. It must have been a dream after all. I wanted to believe it so much. I wanted Him to come." Two great tears welled up in his eyes so that he could hardly see.

But suddenly it seemed the room was full of people. The old beggar, the young woman with the baby, all the people he had spoken to and helped that day.

As they passed they whispered, one by one. "Didn't you see me?" "I was here, Papa Ben." It sounded like the voice of Jesus.

He strained to see but all he saw were the people around him. "Where are you, Jesus?" He called. "Is that you? I can't see you."

Then, just as the night before the same voice spoke. "I was hungry and you gave me food. I was thirsty and you gave me water. I was cold and you took me in. These people you have helped today…all the time you were helping them , you were helping Me. For that is the true spirit of Christmas."

Papa Ben looked around at the room full of people.

"Well, well," he said. "He came. He came after all. Jesus came after all."

Papa Ben shook his head and the sparkle came back to his eyes.

****

911

The rain slick streets made driving nearly impossible. It was the worst storm of a year of bad storms. The ambulance, its siren screaming, approached the intersection throwing sheets of water from its wheels. Andrew, the driver, needed all of his experience to navigate the flooded streets.

Fortunately the drivers, alerted by the sound of the siren, had pulled to the side of the road to allow him a clear path. There was an intersection just ahead so Andrew punched the warbler on his siren and entered the intersection. Suddenly, from out of the sheeting rain, came a pick-up truck, moving too fast to stop in time.

The man in the truck slammed on his brakes as Andrew punched the accelerator and tore through the intersection, barely clearing the pick-up which was now skidding across the intersection and crashed into a row of bushes that absorbed his momentum and brought the truck to a stop. The driver sat quietly, his head on his arms, hunched over the steering wheel.

The ambulance continued down the street toward the

freeway. The emergency call had come in just minutes before. There had been an accident on the section of highway that skirted the small town of Whitman. Andrew, and his partner Sam had been working this shift together for about a year and a half. Sam had been a driver in the big city to the North but grew tired of the stress and emotional strain and resigned to take a position here in Whitney. Andrew was hoping to be able to land a job in a big city where there would be more excitement than he was experiencing here. They were the only ambulance crew assigned to the small hospital and most calls were just routine. Taking elderly folks to the doctor, picking up someone for a trip to the clinic, and washing the ambulance was a little too tame for Andrew.

Sam was different. After 25 years as a big city ambulance driver the little town of Whitman was just what he needed. And he didn't miss the emergency calls for people maimed in an accident, victims of a crime or children hit by cars on the street. He was tired of the stress, and heartbreak of the job. Tired of watching people die while they worked to save them.

Andrew and Sam talked about those things when not racing to a 911 call.

The ambulance slowed to a stop as they saw the

carnage on the highway. It was a seven car pile up and there were bodies strewn across the roadway, some people staggering around with blood streaming from their heads, and others motionless in the seats of the cars.

Andrew and Sam jumped from the ambulance and began to triage the victims, and as other units began to arrive, directed them to the various injured to begin treatment.

Andrew lost track of time. His first injury was a possible broken neck, which he immobilized, and set up transport to the hospital. Then it was lacerations to be sutured, bleeding to be stopped, nerves to be calmed, broken bones to be immobilized and a dozen other needs.

Sam was equally as busy and, with his extensive experience in the big city he handled everything with a calm spirit that began to calm down the injured, encourage the medics, and administer treatment quickly and efficiently.

As the last hospital bound victim was on their way to the hospital Andrew and Sam sat down on the back of their ambulance, totally exhausted. "Ever have anything like this happen at your last job?" Andrew asked Sam. When Sam didn't answer Andrew turned and noticed tears sliding down his dirty cheeks. "Are you alright?" he asked.

"Every day, Andrew, every day." Sam answered quietly. "There are a lot of accidents in the city. More cars, more people, more chances for accidents." Sam looked up, "But the hardest things are those that cause innocent people to be harmed. I've seen it all, and that's why I left."

"Was it just one thing or all the things combined?"

"At first I handled it pretty well. But the first time I responded to a murder and saw that it was a child something snapped. From then on it just seemed to get more and more heavy. It got so I couldn't sleep at night. I would see the faces of those I treated. Some of which I held in my arms as they died.."

Andrew listened closely. Sam had never talked about his time in the city. It was important to Andrew because he wanted to know what it was like working as an EMT somewhere besides little old Whitman.

"I started drinking." Sam continued. "It was the only way I could forget. Pretty soon it started to affect my job, and my relationships. Wife left me and took the kids. Lost my home, everything. Finally the ambulance company had had enough of my poor performance and fired me."

"Sam," Andrew said. "I had no idea.

"Well, it isn't something I am proud of so I don't talk about it much, if at all."

"So, how did you wind up here in Whitman?"

Sam sat silently for a moment before he began to speak softly. "I was alone one night, sitting in my small apartment with a bottle of booze. Andrew, I never felt so miserable and worthless. I decided that I had no reason to keep on living. I went to my dresser and took out this old .38 revolver that I had been hanging on to since my dad gave it to me when I was a kid before he died. I made sure it was loaded and then went back into the living room and sat down on the sofa." Sam hesitated, stared into space for a long moment, and then started to cry.

Andrew didn't know what to say. He was shocked by all that Sam had said and now, to see him crying was really tough to watch.

"Sorry, Andrew," Sam choked through his tears. "It still breaks my heart to think how far I had fallen."

Andrew waited for Sam to speak.

"I put the gun to my head, closed my eyes and pulled the trigger. Nothing happened. I pulled it again. Nothing. Six times I pulled that trigger and six times nothing happened."

"What?" Andrew said. "Six times and nothing happened?"

"Six times. Six times I pulled that trigger and it never fired once. I threw the gun across the room and fell on the floor sobbing. I was a total failure. I couldn't even kill myself."

Andrew put his arm around Sam. "There must have been a reason for all of this. There must have been something that kept you from killing yourself."

"There was," Sam said. "There was. It was my Dad. He kept me from doing it."

"Wait a minute, Sam." You said your dad was dead."

"He was, is, has been for ten years."

"So how could he stop you from killing yourself if he had been dead for ten years?"

Sam had stopped crying and as he looked up Andrew

saw a calmness in his eyes. Almost a peaceful look. Far from the anguish of a few minutes ago. He waited for him to speak.

"My Dad gave me that pistol when I was about ten years old. He was dying from the cancer that finally took him. As he handed me the gun he said, 'Son, I have never used this gun. I want you to have it but I hope you will never have to use it, too.' So I put the gun away and the first time I ever wanted to use it was when I wanted to kill myself."

"Okay," Andrew said. "but how can you say your Dad stopped you from doing it?"

"After a few minutes of sobbing I crawled over to where the gun lay against the wall. I held it a long time, just looking at it. Why had it not fired I asked myself. I slowly began to remove the bullets until I saw the reason why it wouldn't fire."

"Why," Andrew blurted out. "What was the reason it wouldn't fire?"

"There was no firing pin. My Dad must have removed it before giving it to me. No firing pin, Andrew. He stopped me from killing myself ten years ago when he gave me that pistol."

"Then what happened?"

"I sat for a long time on the floor just looking at the gun. I felt defeated. But I had another thought that crept into my mind. I had another chance."

"To kill yourself?"

"No, to do something with this life I had been given. Instead of lying on the floor with out life, I was sitting against the wall with life. A life I could change. A life I could rebuild. A life I could do something with."

Andrew was speechless. He finally saw Sam for who he really was. A man who had looked death in the eye and death blinked.

"I got up from the floor," Sam continued, "went to the cabinet and threw out all the booze, put the gun back in the drawer, took a shower and set about rebuilding my life. Took me five years but I got my wife and kids back, got a house over on the North side of town and got this great ambulance job, with a really great partner. All because my Dad removed the firing pin from that old .38 revolver."

Sam's beeper buzzed.

"C'mon Andrew, duty calls." He said as he jumped up,

closed the ambulance doors and went running to the cab and climbed in with Andrew close behind him.

****

The Clock Maker

He was a clockmaker.

The finest in all Germany they said.

His masterpieces had won awards and acclaim through out the world. He lived alone, unmarried, and devoted himself entirely to the creation of his clocks. They were his family, his friends, his lovers. They were his life.

His name was Gunter Schable and he was an outstanding clockmaker. Unfortunately, he was also a Jew.

When the persecutions began his fame as a clockmaker did him no good at all. Because of his fame he was one of the first to be arrested. Early one morning the Brown

Shirts crashed through the front door of his shop and dragged him into the street. As he lay on the cobblestones he watched as they destroyed his beautiful clocks. Pushing them over, smashing the glass on the front, ripping the pendulums off and destroying the intricately designed faces. And all the while laughing and taunting him.

When the shop had been completely destroyed they dragged him to a truck and threw him in the back, along with several of his Jewish neighbors.

Soon they were at Auschwitz. That was the beginning of six years of hell as he watched friends, relatives and others marched to the gas chambers. Each day he waited for them to come for him but, through God's grace he was still there when the Americans liberated it.

He left Germany, then. First to France, and then to the United States. His hands, that had once created beautiful clocks, were gnarled and twisted from the brutality in the camp. Building clocks was now impossible. So he found work as a janitor, and dreamed of those days when the world gasped in awe at his clocks.

But he also dreamed the dreams of Auschwitz. Nearly

thirty five years later he still woke screaming from the horrors he had seen. Horrors he could never forget. He could still see the faces of the guards as they tortured and killed his people. Jews.

One morning, as he left his home for a walk to clear the dreams from his mind he saw a large crowd of people. Ordinarily he would avoid crowds because they terrified him. But there was something different about this crowd. They were jeering and shouting at several brown shirted men that the group had surrounded.

As he worked his way through the group he found himself face to face with the most hated symbol of his life. The brown shirts were wearing Swastikas on their sleeves.

Fear twisted at his guts.

"Not here, not in America. I will not live through this again. He grabbed at the men, attacked them, beating his gnarled fists agains the hated symbols of his agony. His action seemed to trigger the crowd and they surged forward, striking, and cursing and hitting and kicking the men.

One of the brown shirts hit Gunther, knocking him to the ground. He struggled to get up but the crowd was in a frenzy now. He fell again. Then someone kicked him, and he felt a jarring blow to his head.

When he regained consciousness he found himself in the hospital. A young doctor, standing by his bedside, smiled and asked him how he managed to be involved in the battle. "To be a Jew is to always be in the battle" he sighed.

But he felt good. After thirty five years he felt good. He would never let the brown shirts do it again. He would fight them now. An old man, yes, but now a fighter. No more terror. The old clockmaker finally slept. But he would never dream of prison camps again.

****

SMILE

It was a strange disease. Well, some called it a disease. Some called it a mental condition and others just had no idea what to call it.

It hit the city in the Spring and, at first, every one just thought it was Spring Fever. But it got worse.

It started with smiles, just smiles, on everyones face. At first it was on the faces of those who smiled often. But soon even the craggiest, hard bitten face wore a big grin.

And people started being nice to each other. Not just in passing, but in all things. Men held the door for ladies, gave up their seats on the bus and complimented them on how nice they looked.

The women, in turn, forgot all about being liberated and thanked the men. Conversation became the fad of the masses. Television began to fade from the public affection, as did cell phones, and newspapers were forced to print only good news, because that's all there was to report, and their circulation went up 100% Crime rapidly fell into disrepute and police officers spent most of their time directing traffic.

One of the biggest changes was in politics. Politicians began to tell the truth about everything. Initially you could see their confusion when all they could say was truthful. But, within a few weeks there was a complete revamp of the political structure of the country.

People began to help each other. Welfare was forgotten. People gave a days work for a days wage and the Union halls closed down. Banks closed, too. No one had the time to save their money. They were too busy helping people and putting it into projects like the clean-up of the environment.

The United Staes became just that. United. And it shocked the rest of the world. Russia threatened an all out invasion if America didn't straighten up and get back in the arms race.

America ignored the threat.

Soon America began to withdraw all her troops from overseas. The Army began a complete renovation of the country. The Navy began an extensive clean-up of the coastal areas, and also the inland waterways.

The Air Force spent its time flying crews around the country to help with the harvests, fight forest fires and rebuild structures that had fallen into disrepair over the years.

Other countries, watching this transformation, began to panic. Foreign powers began to increase the size of their armed forces and attempted to isolated themselves from America, lest the "disease" affect them.

It did no good. Japan was the first to discover that people were smiling more and becoming even more gracious than they, as Japanese, usually were.

Panic took hold.

Scientists in Russia and China worked furiously to block the epidemic from infecting their countries. European countries also worked feverishly to create some sort of defense against the "disease".

Too late.

One by one the nations began to fall. And the advancement of mankind was phenominal. No more wars. No more poverty. No more hatred. No sadness. Only a joy that invaded every aspect of life on the planet.

Two thousand years later the Intergalactic Agency for Peace and Love made contact with the people of earth and explained to them what they had done so many years ago.

Nobody believed them.

****

Midred Hannibel

Mildred Hannibel loved to be called Millie by all her friends. And she had hundreds. Unfortunately, all these friends were visible only to Millie. It was really too bad that her friends in the Rest Home couldn't see them. She felt that they would all have enjoyed each other.

Millie had been at the Rest Home for years. She couldn't remember how many but it must have been at least twenty to hear her tell it. Actually it was only twelve and she had her last visit from her children on Mother's Day five years ago. They didn't come around anymore, telling themselves that she was senile and didn't recognize them anyway. But Millie knew. In her poor, befuddled mind, she knew. And that is why she made so many new friends.

Millie met a new friend every day, and spent the whole day with them. They helped her tidy her room, ate with her at mealtimes and went for walks with her around the grounds.

Abigail Sansome was with her the day she walked away from the Home.

Millie Hadn't noticed she had walked so far. She was so busy carrying on a conversation with Abigail that she lost track of time. Of course, as she walked down the street talking with Abigail the passersby just shook their heads and smiled.

It was late afternoon when she realized that they were both hopelessly lost. And when her companion didn't seem to care Millie began to shout and wave her arms. Which drew some surprised looks from other pedestrians.

She finally decided that, because Abigail seemed so unconcerned, that it was up to her to get them home.

But she couldn't remember the name or address of the Home. So, she and Abigail walked up one street, then down another for nearly an hour without recognizing anything familiar. Exhausted the found a bus bench and sat down to catch their breath.

Suddenly a bus swung to the curb and the doors whooshed open. A friendly voice called to her inviting her and Abigail to come aboard. At first she hesitated but when she saw the kind, smiling face of the driver she felt better about it and, without waiting for Abigail, she climbed aboard the bus.

She fumbled with the tiny purse she always carried with her and, with the help of the driver paid her fare, and Abigails. The driver seemed to think it was strange that she was paying for two. But Millie just turned and took a seat at the front of the bus, with Abigail next to her.

As she watched the streets and buildings whizzing by she began to get worried again. Nothing looked familiar, and Abigail was no help. She was pouting because Millie had gotten angry with her. Having no idea where to get off the bus she stood up and exited at the next stop.

She was lost.

Oh my, Millie had never been lost before and she started to cry. Abigail began to cry, too. What would they do now? It was getting late and Millie grew more frightened.

"There you are, Millie" she heard a familiar voice. "I have been looking all over for you." It was Dr. Lianne, from the Home. The doctor put her arm around Millie and helped her into the car. As she settled comfortably into the back seat she felt very tired, but happy.

However, she told herself, that would be the last time she and Abigail ever went walking together.

****

Money Isn't Everything

Life was good for Michelle. She had married well, she thought. Her husband was industrious, handsome and successful. They had a big house, two awesome cars, and all the luxuries she could ever want or need.

It was about the second year of the marriage that her husband seemed to grow more distant every day. "I work hard," he told her when she asked why he was away from home so much. "You have everything a woman could want. A beautiful house, a great car, plenty of clothes and shoes. A maid to clean the house, and a chef to prepare great meals."

"Great meals," she interrupted him. "That you are

never home to eat. A great big house with only me in it. And a great car that I can drive wherever I want to go, by myself."

"I'm sorry that all I have provided for you just makes you unhappy." He said.

"What makes me unhappy is that I never see you. I love you and want to spend time with you but work comes first." She began to cry. "I get lonely."

"I get lonely for you, too." he said softly. "But to have all we have means that I have to sacrifice our time together to stay on top." He took her in his arms and held her close. "Try and understand that what I do takes all of my time. And for us to live like this I have to do it. Now, dry your eyes and head up to bed. I have to leave for a time but will see you in the morning." And he turned to the door and walked away.

She stood watching as he put on his jacket, picked up his briefcase, blew her a kiss and walked out the door. She still stood there as she heard his car drive away. Then she turned slowly and climbed the stairs to their bedroom.

He wasn't there in the morning when she awoke. It didn't surprise her. As she lay in the bed she began to think to herself. "Well, if he must work so hard to keep all we have, then I intend to enjoy it."

That began a new change of life for her. She began to buy new clothes. Some were quite revealing. And she began to attend more of the parties that those in her society threw almost endlessly.

St the parties she found that a little too much to drink made her feel a bit less depressed and, since she was a beautiful woman she had many admirers. But she was careful not to go too far lest she lose her husband.

She spoke glowingly of him to everyone she met. But it was a little uncomfortable trying to explain why he was never at the parties with her. She would just laugh and say he was a hard worker. Most just smiled and nodded their head.

This went on for more than a year and, even the parties and drinking and laughing did little to lessen her depression and loneliness. She was still in love with her husband and was happy when they were together. But those times grew even less and less.

Then one day two police officers show up at her door looking for her husband. She doesn't understand but she gives them the address of his office. "I'm sorry," one of the policemen says. "We have just left that address and it is a vacant warehouse."

"I don't understand," she said. "That is where his office has always been."

"Do you have any idea where he might be?" The officer asked.

"If he isn't there I have no idea where he might be. That is the only address I have for his office." Michelle was beginning to panic. "What do you want with him?" She blurted out, tears forming in her eyes.

"We just need to ask him some questions," The officer said, handing her a card. "Please have him contact us as soon as you can." And they turned and left.

Michelle hurried to the phone and called her husband's number. "This number is no longer in service." a voice said. "Please check the number and try again"

"No longer in service," she screamed. "No longer in service. My God, now what do I do?"

Just then she heard the garage door open. She ran to the door into the garage, threw it opened and there was her husband looking uncomfortable. "Jerry," she yelled. "What do the police want with you?"

"Shut up." He growled. "And get out of the way." Pushing past her he went to his office and began stacking piles of folders and papers on his desk. He went to the safe, opened it and Michelle was surprised to see the stacks of bills it held.

Grabbing handfuls of the money he began to stuff it in his briefcase. There were also documents and other papers that he also crammed into the case.

"Jerry," Michelle yelled, "What are you doing? What is going on?"

Her husband didn't answer but finished emptying the safe and, grabbing the pile of folders from the desk started for the garage. "Don't follow me," he growled loudly. "You have nothing to do with this."

With that he climbed into his car and opened the garage door. To his surprise there were two police cars parked in the driveway, blocking his escape.

It was only a matter of minutes until they had her husband, all the folders, and his briefcase in one of the police cars. The car with him in it left. One of the officers from the other patrol car came up to her. "Please do not leave this house." He said. "There will be a team of detectives here in about ten minutes with a search warrant."

"A search warrant?" Michelle whispered. "Can you please tell me what is going on? What has my husband done?"

"You will have to discuss that with the detectives." He answered just as three more cars pulled into the driveway.

The detectives were very thorough. Also messy. By the time they were through the house looked like it had been struck by a tornado. And all time they were working they ignored her questions. She had finally had enough. Screaming at the top of her lungs she demanded."WHAT IN THE NAME OF GOD IS GOING ON!!!"

The detectives stopped and quietly spoke to her. "Mrs Parker, this is a serious matter which we are not allowed to discuss with you. Someone will be here soon to inform you of the situation."

"Should I call a lawyer?" she asked.

"If you like. It might not be a bad idea."

And with that Michelle's life was turned upside down

The next few weeks were a nightmare. Endless

meetings, court appearances, lawyer conferences and newspaper reporters invading her privacy daily.

As the days went on it became clear to Michelle just what was going on. Her husband was not the man she thought he was. The big house, the fancy cars, all the expensive things were bought with other people's money. Her husband was in the business of defrauding people of their hard earned money through bogus stock deals, and non-existent investments.

As the legal turmoil went on it was decided that she was not involved in any of his deals and so she was removed from the case. She still went to court every day, sat in on the proceedings and grew more and more depressed. How could this be the man she loved?

The court proceeding continued for three months with her husband found guilty and sentenced to prison. All of their elegant possessions were taken and sold to compensate the lawyers and those people defrauded by her husband. She had nothing but a small savings account that she had before her marriage.

It allowed her to rent a studio apartment while she looked for work. But it was tough getting a job because of all the publicity surrounding the court proceedings. She finally was able to find work in a Dry Cleaning plant where she was always out of sight among the machines.

Her fancy friends wanted nothing to do with her.

One evening, after an especially grueling day at the plant she sat quietly in her apartment with a cup of tea and began to think about all that had gone on. She suddenly realized that she felt a sense of peace. A release from an intolerable situation. A calmness. And she began to think about the future. Her future.

In one of her visits to her husband she mentioned a new start when he was released. His answer surprised her.

"Right, a new start," he said. "A new location, a new name, a fresh start, and fresh suckers to relieve of their money" He laughed.

As she looked carefully at her partner of ten years she wondered if it was possible to live that long with someone and not really know them. She turned and left the prison. As she walked to the bus stop, her car had gone with the rest of their things, she understood what she must do.

There must be a new start, a new name and a new place. But only for her. Perhaps someday she would find the love she has wanted for so long.

As the bus pulled away she never looked back at the prison.

****

How The Wino Saved The World

Everything about John was rotten.

His dilapidated canvas shoes, rummage sale pants and shirt, faded brown jacket and ragged underwear. Even the few teeth that clung to his sodden gums were rotten. He lived, off and on, at the Midnight Mission and he never took a bath, not even for Christmas. No one could stand to get close to him.

In other words, John was a mess, and not at all the type to save the world.

But he did.

I met John one Summer evening a while back when I was a little down on my luck and found he was a good man to share a bottle of wine with. He and I spent many an hour drinking whatever we could scrape together the money for and swapping tales.

One warm afternoon John and I were perched on a hillside overlooking Dodger Stadium when he started his toothless cackle. I was sitting upwind, a precaution I always took when we were together, so his breath didn't stop me from asking him what was so funny.

Well, the story he told me is nearly impossible to believe but I'll tell it to you the same way he told it and you can decide for yourself. I'll leave out the occasional belch or the loud and odorous emanations from his backside which were a part of his normal conversation. They won't be missed.

One Sunday evening, about January or so he was alone with the remains of a Saturday night drunk, folded loosely in a doorway trying to keep out of the rain that was dousing the city. Water wasn't his favorite liquid.

Being concerned with keeping dry he didn't take much notice of the two dark shapes that stopped in front of him. People were always stopping to look at John, but they never stayed too long, the smell was more than most folks could stand.

But these two wouldn't go away, which made John even more uncomfortable than the rain.

He was about to tell them to get out of his doorway when one of the two reached out his hand. In it was a shiny object that John couldn't clearly see.

The hand touched the shiny object to John's head and he blacked out.

The surface he was laying on was cold and hard and certainly not the doorway. John slowly opened his eyes. He lay in the middle of a large room, with smooth walls and a bright overhead light.

Now, John had woken up in some strange places in his past. Once, he said, he even woke up in a lion's cage at the Los Angeles Zoo. He always laughed at that. Said it was only the Lion's keen sense of smell that kept him from being eaten.

But this was like no place he had ever been before. The walls, to John's dismay, were clean and bright and there were no windows, or even a door, anywhere to be seen.

He thought that he must be in the hospital again but

that thought was quickly replaced by one more urgent. He had to go, bad. But where? Well, actually that particular problem was one he solved easily. He went wherever he could.

So, John sat up on the table, swung his legs over the side and stood up. There were no visible doors anywhere along the smooth, shiny walls, so a bathroom seemed unlikely. John staggered over to one of the corners, reached out a hand to steady himself but drew back at the last second. He couldn't bring himself to touch anything as clean as that wall. Spreading his feet for balance he unzipped his pants and began to take care of business, spraying the smooth finish.

He nearly messed his pants when the siren went off.

Behind him he heard a door opening and turned to see several almost human shapes scurrying toward the mess he had made. They made a point not to get too close to John as they began spraying the area with a purplish spray that quickly had the wall and floor as spotless as before. John hoped, very much, that they weren't going to spray him with that stuff.

He turned and looked at several of the group that stood a respectable distance away. They were a foot or so taller than he and wore loose garments that barely touched the floor. Their heads and faces were hidden by hoods that swept up from their shoulders but John caught a glimpse of one as it turned and saw a long, crooked nose, a wide mouth and…three eyes!

The two with the sprayer were moving slowly toward him as he began to back away trying to get as much distance between him and that spray. He flattened himself against the far wall of the room. John leaped away from the wall just fast enough to avoid the purple spray as the siren began to scream again,

In his fear and confusion John stumbled toward the other group that stood near the center of the room. This caused them to scatter in all directions, a reaction similar to that of most people when they saw him coming. One of the group drew an object from the folds of his garment and shot John in the chest.

It wasn't the strangeness of his surroundings, or the fact that he was now held securely to a small table by a force he couldn't see. What bothered John as he awoke was the fact that he was… .sober.

Not clear headed, or alert. Just sober. And he didn't like it at all.

He was able to move only his head and eyes, but there

was nothing much to see. He was in a room somewhat smaller than the one he had been in before. But it was just as doorless, just as windowless, and just as clean.

John began to shout at the top of his voice. He cursed, he pleaded, he raved, he threatened. But all he heard were his own words echoing back at him from the gleaming walls. John stopped, took a breath, and waited for the noise to subside.

His head ached. He wasn't sure if it was a hangover, or the shouting that started it. He only knew he had to do something to get out of there.

Then, like a glimmer of light at the end of a seldom used hallway, John got an idea.

Turning his head to the right he cleared his throat and spit a great gob against the nearest wall.

The siren screamed again.

A door, just out of his sight, opened and the cleanup crew raced in and went to work with the purple spray. John began to shout again. He called them every name he could think of, and he knew quite a few, and threatened all sorts of mayhem. No use. They finished their cleaning and raced out of the room.

John was yelling for them, or anyone, to come back when he heard the door slide open again. One of the figures in the long robe walked in carrying something. John could only watch helplessly as the tall, robed shape placed a shiny cap on his filthy matted hair. His skin began to crawl from the touch of the cap. The tall robed figure turned away with a visible shudder and left the room. John decided they didn't like him any more than he liked them.

Next several of his captors entered the room and arranged themselves in a semi-circle around the foot of the table. He was worried, he was sober and he was definitely unhappy about the whole thing.

One of the group spoke.

John's surprise was total. They were speaking English. He tried to clear his head of the pain and confusion as he listened to the strange sounding voice in his mind.

The cap he was wearing, the speaker told him, was a translating device which would allow them to communicate. They could now understand him, as well. John couldn't speak. And as he listened he grew more, and more uncomfortable.

His captors were from a distant planet in a far solar

system. John never learned where. Their civilization was slowly dying from a population explosion that they were unable to control. The ship that John was on had come to this galaxy searching for a planet suitable for colonization. If conditions were favorable a large group of them would migrate here.

Their time was short and they had chosen John as a typical representative of the people of this planet. He was the first human they had contacted, unfortunately for everyone concerned.

John was to undergo a series of tests to determine the best course of action with the present inhabitants of the planet. If the test were positive the people of Earth would become slaves to this alien race. As the speaker continued John's soggy mind began to clear. By the time the explanation was over John knew he was in big trouble.

After a very animated discussion between the group one of them, reluctantly began to wheel John from the room while the rest followed at a safe distance. His mind was struggling with all he had been told. If these creatures came to earth to stay his drinking days would be over. But how could he stop what he couldn't understand? And what were the tests?

He was helpless. He had no weapons, nothing to fight with. Then his eyes narrowed. There might be a way out of this after all.

John was wheeled into a gleaming laboratory crammed with bewildering banks of equipment. Lights were blinking on what he thought was a control panel and a steady hum filled the room. He was lifted from the table and held motionless while his clothes were removed from his thin body. The technicians shrank from the smell that moved like an invisible wall across the room. It wasn't only his clothes that were rotten.

Placed in a padded chair, and hurriedly strapped down, John watched as thin wires were attached to various parts of his body. Others in the room began to position themselves in front of the banks of instruments.

As the last of the wires were fitted into place John emptied his bowels.

The alarm sounded louder here in the laboratory. Panic was everywhere. A cleaning crew entered the room and recoiled from the smell. They warily approached the odorous pile and, as John was lifted from the chair, doused everything with the purple spray. After a few seconds John was reseated and strapped down again.

The cleaning crew and several of the technicians stood just in front of him. With an unerring aim he began to relieve himself. He caught all of those in front of him before they could move and the siren drowned out any sound they might have made.

The cleaning crew, dripping with urine from their cloaks, sprayed the entire area and then left the room along with the others.

His plan seemed to be working. But he had no idea how long he could keep it up. But one thing was reassuring. He didn't have to worry about that spray. He never saw it used on anything but walls and equipment. What a relief. They probably had some sort of shower or bath to clean themselves.

The thought made him shiver.

In a short while the group of technicians returned and began to set up for the series of tests again. John waited. Just as things seemed to be getting underway he emptied his bowels again. Then later he relieved himself, again spraying anyone within range. As the technicians continued to perform the tests John used everything in his arsenal. He broke wind, spit, urinated and emptied his bowels until he was totally exhausted. With each salvo the alarm screamed, and pandemonium grew worse. But finally John was totally exhausted and out of ammo. His mind groped to find another means of resistance when the one who spoke to him before entered the room.

The translating cap was again placed on his head. As the leader spoke John was lifted from his chair. He listened in dismay as he was told the results of the tests. In spite of his actions they had been able to complete enough of the procedures to determine there would be little or no trouble in subduing the inhabitants of the planet. John's heart sank. He had failed.

But the speaker wasn't finished. They had also decided that living on the same planet with such a dirty, uncontrollable, miserable race would be unbearable for them. They would look elsewhere for a home.

John was so relieved he broke wind. The speaker, who was standing directly in front of John, had to be helped from the room.

John's clothes were replaced and he was once more seated in the chair. A technician stepped in front of him and touched his forehead with a short wand and the lights blinked out in his mind.

John woke up in the doorway where he was found. He

would have chalked the whole thing up to a bad dream except for one thing.

He was sober.

He stood and looked around him. The rain had washed the streets clean and the sun was slowly lighting the Eastern sky. It would be a beautiful day.

John hitched up his pants and hurried off to get drunk.

He had come to the end of his story. Emptying the bottle of wine he stood up, and without a word, staggered down the hillside.

I never saw John again after that day on the hill. Things got better for me and, I guess, worse for him. Several months later I learned from one of the residents at the Midnight Mission that he had fallen into the swollen Los Angeles river during a heavy rain and drowned.

Knowing how John felt about water, that must have been an even more frightening experience than the night he saved the world.

The End

Made in the USA
Columbia, SC
08 May 2019